TAKE ACTION!

EAT SMART!

By Kirsty Holmes

BookLife
PUBLISHING

©2020
BookLife Publishing Ltd.
King's Lynn
Norfolk PE30 4LS

ISBN: 978-1-83927-106-9

Written by:
Kirsty Holmes

Edited by:
Emilie Dufresne

Designed by:
Brandon Mattless

Words that look like **this** can be found in the glossary on page 24.

PHOTO CREDITS

CONTENTS

Page 4	No Plan(et) B
Page 6	A Big Problem
Page 8	Problem: Food
Page 10	Waste Not, Want Not
Page 12	Go Meat Free!
Page 14	Seasons Eatings
Page 16	Go Local
Page 18	Grow Your Own
Page 20	Natural Nosh
Page 22	Choose to Reuse
Page 24	Glossary and Index

NO PLAN(ET) B

Planet Earth provides us with food, water and shelter. It really is a good home – it has everything we need.

If you could go anywhere on Earth, where would you go?

There isn't an endless supply of the things we need in order to live. If we don't take care of these things, they will run out.

It's really important that we take care of the things we need.

A BIG PROBLEM

Many grown-ups haven't been taking very good care of our home.

The way we farm is harming **ecosystems**.

Pesticides are bad for our land.

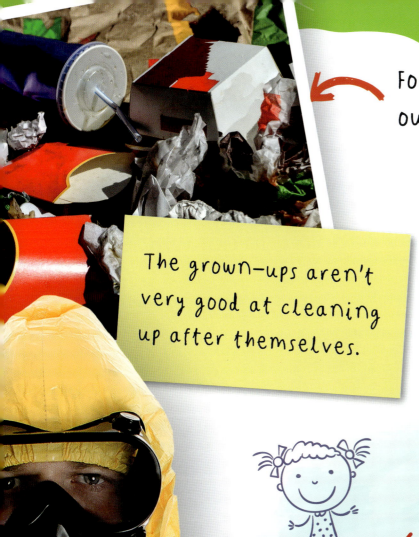

Food packaging is <u>polluting</u> our ecosystems.

The grown-ups aren't very good at cleaning up after themselves.

There is lots to do, and that can seem scary. But the important thing is to believe that if we try, we can change things.

You might be thinking:

"What can I do about it?"

"I'm just a kid!"

Turns out, you can do a lot!

It's time to **TAKE ACTION!**

PROBLEM: FOOD

With over 7 billion people living on the planet today, there are more mouths to feed than ever. Many people can eat whatever food they want, at any time of year.

What's your favourite food?

This might seem great, but the way these foods are made and grown has bad effects on our **environment**. It also uses a lot of **resources**.

TAKE ACTION! It's time to think about eating smarter.

WASTE NOT, WANT NOT

Each year, as much as one–third of all food **produced** around the world is wasted. These are the world's most wasted foods.

Bread

Milk

Meats

Fresh vegetables and potatoes

BRILLIANT WAYS TO REDUCE WASTE

1. Portion control!

Only take what you are certain you will eat at mealtimes.

2. Store it right!

Make sure you wrap leftovers and store them correctly.

3. Eat leftovers!

Eating leftover food reduces food waste.

GO MEAT FREE!

Raising animals for their meat and milk is bad for the environment. One of the simplest ways to make a difference is to cut down on food that comes from animals.

Cheese

Red meat

Milk

Fish

Eggs

Poultry

Some people choose to become vegetarian or vegan. Vegetarians don't eat meat, fish or poultry. Vegans don't eat these things either, but they also don't eat or use anything that comes from an animal, such as cheese and milk.

Always talk to your grown-ups before making any changes to your **diet**.

SEASONS EATINGS

For a long time, most people's diets would mostly have been made up of things that were available near them and **in season** at the time.

Pumpkins are in season in autumn. It's a great time for pumpkin soup!

Eating food in season means that your food won't have to travel as far to reach you because it can be grown locally instead of in another country. This is better for the planet.

Summer is the season for delicious fruits and berries.

PICK YOUR OWN STRAWBERRIES

TAKE ACTION! Find out what foods are in season near you this month.

GO LOCAL

Foods that aren't in season travel farther, which uses up more **fuel**. The distance food travels is called its food miles.

The more food miles an item has, the worse it is for the environment.

Choosing to eat foods that are grown locally means we don't have to use as much fuel to transport them from other places. One of the best places to find local food can be your local farmers' market.

How many vegetables on this market stall can you name?

GROW YOUR OWN

It doesn't get more local than your own back garden! Growing your own fruits, vegetables and herbs is the best way to make sure your food is local, seasonal and has no food miles at all!

You don't have to have a big garden to grow your own food. You can grow some herbs and vegetables indoors, and many things can be grown in bags, containers and even hanging baskets!

Some things can be grown in greenhouses even through the winter!

Greenhouse

Hanging basket for herbs

NATURAL NOSH

When you go to the supermarket, help your grown-ups make smart shopping choices. Look for things that are labelled 'organic' as these are grown without harmful pesticides.

Can you find any locally grown foods?

Choose loose, unwrapped items that aren't in plastic packaging where you can. When you buy loose fruit and vegetables, it is easier to only get what you need to reduce food waste.

Plastic packaging is bad for the environment. Buying loose helps you to cut down your waste.

CHOOSE TO REUSE

Make sure you always take a **<u>reusable</u>** bag when you go shopping. Bringing your own bag means a plastic bag won't be used.

TAKE ACTION! <u>Remind</u> your grown-ups to take reusable bags when you go shopping.

Some shops let you refill your own bottles and jars with the food and products that you need so that you don't make any waste when buying things.

Have you ever been to a shop like this one?

GLOSSARY

diet	the kinds of food that a person or animal usually eats
ecosystems	the communities of living things and the environment they live in
environment	the natural world
fuel	something that can be used to make energy or power something
in season	grown and able to buy during the current time of year
pesticides	chemicals used to kill insects that may harm plants and crops
polluting	when something harmful or poisonous is introduced to the environment
poultry	chickens, turkeys and other birds that are raised for their meat and eggs
produced	made
resources	useful materials that are created by nature
reusable	able to be used over and over again

INDEX

food miles 16, 18
fruit 15, 18, 21
growing 9, 15, 17–20
packaging 7, 21

plastic 21–22
shopping 20–23
vegan 13
vegetables 10,

17–19, 21
vegetarian 13
waste 10–11, 21, 23